Robin's
Impossible, Crazy Idea

Sylvia Gunnery

Illustrated by Jill Quinn

Pottersfield Press, Lawrencetown Beach, Nova Scotia, Canada

National Library of Canada Cataloguing in Publication Data

Gunnery, Sylvia
      Robin's impossible, crazy idea
      ISBN 1-895900-46-8
I. Quinn, Jill   II. Title.
PS8563.U575R62 2001   jC813'.54   C2001-902027-9
PZ7.G9725Ro 2001

Editor: Carol McDougall

Pottersfield Press gratefully acknowledges the ongoing support of the Nova Scotia Department of Culture and Tourism, Cultural Affairs Division, as well as The Canada Council for the Arts. We acknowledge the financial support of the Government of Canada through the Book Publishing Industry Development Program for our publishing activities.

Pottersfield Press
83 Leslie Road
East Lawrencetown
Nova Scotia, Canada, B2Z 1P8
Website: www.pottersfieldpress.com

To order, phone 1-800-NIMBUS9 (1-800-646-2879)

Printed in Canada

For Sydney, Lily, and Des.
— S.G.

This is for Pam, a wonderful friend and teacher.
— J.Q.B.

- TWO POINTS OFF FOR EVERY SPELLING ERROR.
- NO COPYING THE WORK OF OTHERS.
- NO CHEWING GUM.

Chapter One

Robin was not whistling happily into the spring air, soft and warm around her face. She was not whistling because she could see no reason to be cheerful. All the way from her house at the edge of the sea to the bus stop beside the Crescent Beach General Store, she stared down at her own sneakers plodding along. When the bus wheezed to a stop, Robin got on without even saying good morning to Mrs. Brighten, the bus driver.

School wasn't school anymore. Not the way it used to be before grade four. Before Ms. Beetroot. She was a stern, solid woman who was as old as Ernest Lee Elementary School itself.

She had rules on the classroom door:

REMOVE WET BOOTS

NO FOOD OR DRINK IN CLASS

BE PREPARED WITH PAPER, PENCILS, AND ERASER.

She had rules on the blackboard:

NO BORROWING

NO TALKING

NO EXCUSES.

And she had rules on the bulletin board beside the pencil sharpener:

TWO POINTS OFF FOR EVERY SPELLING ERROR

NO COPYING THE WORK OF OTHERS

NO CHEWING GUM.

It seemed as if no one at home really understood why Robin felt so dreary about going to school every day. Often, as the family ate supper and talked about the ordinary things of everyone's day, she would describe how being in grade four was no fun because of Ms. Beetroot.

Her mother told her that a teacher always tried to do what was best for the students.

Her father told her that she was in a higher grade now and had to settle down.

Her grandfather told her that her school days were the happiest days of her life.

Her older sister said, "I warned you. Watch out for Beetroot."

After making all the regular pick-ups along the winding seaside road, the bus slowed, stopped, then rumbled into the schoolyard. Robin braced herself for another day of rules, rules, rules, building up around her like brick walls.

She glanced out the smudgy window to the place where Ms. Beetroot always stood frowning across the paved schoolyard when the bus deposited all those responsibilities in front of her. Suddenly, Robin's eyes widened in disbelief. Every pair of eyes on the bus was captured by the same strange sight.

Chapter Two

A juggler – yes! – standing on the school steps, knees bent, arms in mechanical motion, eyes holding the three moving objects – one apple, one orange, one pear – as they whirled up and around and down, up and around and down.

The students stepped off the bus slowly, cautiously, as if they might cause the orange, then the pear, and then the apple to fall. They came closer, and closer, staring in disbelief at

the juggler on the Monday morning steps of their ordinary elementary school.

Where was Ms. Beetroot now?

The juggler gave one sudden shout, "Ha!" and caught each object – one, two, three – as they fell in quick, straight lines into his hands. "Welcome, children. My name is Mr. Cunningham. That's cunning as in sly, and ham as in joking around. I will be your substitute grade four teacher for today. Let the show begin!" He turned, opened the large door, and gave a welcoming bow.

The primaries and grade ones shuffled down the hall, trailing after their teachers in uneven lines, looking over their shoulders, unsure of what their eyes had just beheld. The grade twos and grade threes moved unwillingly behind their teachers, wishing they could stay to witness more.

The grade fours stood still as statues.

"Step right up!" grinned Mr. Cunningham, and he marched at the head of the grade four line.

"Your regular teacher, Ms. Beetroot, is not feeling well and has requested a substitute," he announced as the students settled into their seats.

Robin raised her eyebrows up towards the straight line of bright red bangs across her forehead. A whole day without Ms. Beetroot! Was she dreaming?

Chapter Three

Everyone was excited about Mr. Cunningham
– cunning as in sly and ham as in joking
around. He worked his magic through
arithmetic class. The arithmetic books were
piled in teetering stacks and the students were
organized into teams. With shouts from Mr.
Cunningham – "Add two! Subtract three! Divide
by four! Multiply by two!" – the teams raced
frantically back and forth to be the first to
finish with the correct number of books in their
pile.

When it came time for reading, the lights were turned out and curtains pulled shut. Robin volunteered to stand on Ms. Beetroot's desk (oh, if she ever found out) and hold the flashlight, just so, above Mr. Cunningham's balding head as he read about "Strange things done in the midnight sun by the men who moil for gold."

Once, someone (probably Michael) threw a large paper ball at Jason. Mr. Cunningham's long arm shot out and intercepted it like a frog's tongue capturing a fly. He carefully unfurled the ball, perched his glasses on the end of his nose and pretended to be reading a famous poem, "How do I love thee? Let me count the ways." It made everyone laugh, even Michael. (Ms. Beetroot would have held her breath until Michael was out the door and sitting on the red bench in the hallway.)

Chapter Four

That evening, around the supper table, Robin told her father, her mother, her grandfather, and her older sister the unbelievable stories of Mr. Cunningham, the extraordinary substitute for Ms. Beetroot. Everyone laughed, especially when Robin described in great detail how she stood right on the teacher's desk.

Robin felt happy. Things were good again, just like they had been before grade four.

After supper, her older sister washed the dishes while Robin dried them, whistling her usual feeling-happy tune.

"Beetroot'll be back tomorrow," her sister said flatly.

"Maybe she's awfully sick," Robin said. "Maybe –"

"Listen. You gotta face up to it," said her older sister. "Beetroot will be back. No way she'd miss a lot of school, even if someone had to get her there in an ambulance."

Robin couldn't laugh at her sister's lame joke. The truth was the truth. Ms. Beetroot would be frowning on the school steps early in the morning. Her rules would glare down from the classroom door, from the blackboard, and from the bulletin board beside the pencil sharper.

It just isn't fair, thought Robin in despair as she brushed her teeth before going to bed.

She and her sister shared a room with one large window looking out over the sea. Robin's bed was on one side of the window and her sister's was on the other. They could hear the constant hum of the sea and the steady rhythm

17

of waves curling up near the shore, then tumbling onto the pebble beach in front of their home. Sometimes, her sister would read out loud from thick hard-covered books, like *Black Beauty* or *Beautiful Joe.*

"I hate hating school."

"You'll get over it," said her older sister as she switched out the small lamp beside her bed.

"How?" asked Robin, turning off her identical lamp.

"Oh," yawned her sister, "I don't know. Maybe you'll make friends with old Beetroot. She could use a friend." She yawned again and snuggled deep into the downy duvet. Soon she was asleep.

Robin was wide awake. Make friends with Ms. Beetroot? Impossible. Crazy!

But something was creating a sort of itch in her mind. Gradually the itch became an idea that began to form a mental video. Robin could see everything as clearly as if it were happening right before her very eyes. A crazy idea. Impossible!

Chapter Five

The next morning, as she waited for her toast to pop up, Robin began to make a list:

1. find out Ms. Beetroot's birthday
2. collect fifty cents from everybody
3. figure out what present to buy
4. ask people to bring food
5. plan stuff for decorating.

Then, finally, in large capital letters she wrote the most important (and the most difficult) thing of all:

6. TALK EVERYONE INTO HAVING A PARTY FOR MS.
BEETROOT.

Robin felt *different* as she walked towards
the bus stop at the Crescent Beach General
Store that morning. She was not actually happy,
but she had a kind of excitement tingling
through her – an excitement mixed with worry.
It was going to be practically impossible to
convince people that this crazy idea would work.
And what if Ms. Beetroot didn't want a party at
all?

When the bus turned into the schoolyard of
Ernest Lee Elementary School, there was Ms.
Beetroot in her usual spot. But this morning
her frown didn't pull down sharply from the
corners of her mouth and her eyes didn't glare
like darts at the children as they stepped off the
bus.

Ms. Beetroot wore a long plaid scarf
wrapped snugly around her neck, she clasped a
box of tissue against her chest as if it were a
shield, and her long nose was scarlet. She
sneezed a loud CASSSHEW! Then, she blew her
nose noisily into a tissue.

"Gud mording, studends," she said drearily as the grade fours sat timidly in their seats. Ms. Beetroot was mean enough when she was healthy – what ever was she going to be like today when she had a terrible cold?

Robin tucked her list carefully between pages twenty-one and twenty-two of her arithmetic book. Her crazy plan was beginning to seem even more impossible.

Still, she was certain that a party was the only way she could change things at school to the way it used to be before grade four. In fact, Robin was beginning to believe she was a kind of hero about to rescue everyone (even Ms. Beetroot) from those terrible, boring, worrying grade four days.

At recess, she tapped on the classroom door of her grade two teacher, Mrs. Williams. She'd know Ms. Beetroot's birthday. She could be trusted to keep the secret.

"A surprise party!" Mrs. Williams exclaimed. "What a wonderful idea."

"So you don't think Ms. Beetroot will get mad? I mean, there'll be food in the class and noise and – "

"Anyone would be happy to have a surprise party." Then, Mrs. Williams placed her finger on the side of her cheek. "Let me think," she said. "Hazel – I mean, Ms. Beetroot – is very quiet about such things as birthdays, but I do seem to remember . . . Yes. Her birthday is in January. I remember it perfectly because it is the day after Elvis Presley's birthday and his is January 8th."

"January? Oh, no."

"Oh my," said Mrs. Williams. "January. And now it's April. Hmmm. We do have a problem, don't we?"

"Well, thank you for trying to help," said Robin sadly. If she couldn't do something nice for Ms. Beetroot, how could they be friends? How could grade four ever be any different?

"Wait!" said Mrs. Williams just as Robin was closing the classroom door. "Come back," she whispered. "You could still have your party. Only it will be an unbirthday party."

"Just like in *Alice in Wonderland*," said Robin.

Chapter Six

Robin had convinced most of the people in her grade four class that the unbirthday party for Ms. Beetroot was a good idea. Actually, just the word "party" did the trick. Who wouldn't want to have a party instead of doing those long, boring lessons?

Samantha said she'd bring fudge because her father made the very best. Ralph and Roxanne, the twins, would bring jam sandwiches with the crusts cut off. Barbara said her family had lots and lots of lemonade mix and she was sure

she'd be allowed to donate some. Matthew knew how to make peanut butter cookies so he was going to bake a dozen.

Robin volunteered to bring the cake. Inspired by Matthew, she decided she'd even bake it herself. For decorations, Joseph offered to bring a few balloons left over from his parents' New Year's Eve party, along with blue and white streamers that were only slightly tattered. Katie, who always got the highest mark in drawing, said she would create a colourful unbirthday poster.

The day of the party was set: it would be Friday afternoon. Maybe, if Ms. Beetroot had lots of rest and hot soup, she might even be feeling better by then. Maybe if Robin thought and thought and thought, she'd figure out what special gift to get. The unbirthday party was three days away.

That night, Robin pulled the covers up to her chin and stared into the darkness of the bedroom. She was pleased with herself. "You asleep?"

"Almost," said her older sister.

"Guess what?"

"I can't. I'm too tired."

"I'm throwing an unbirthday party for Ms. Beetroot."

"You're kidding, of course."

"I am not. Besides, it was practically your idea."

"Never in a million years would I come up with such a crazy plan."

Robin felt an ocean wave of doubt curl up and crash against her. "But even Mrs. Williams thinks it's a good plan. She said it would be like the unbirthday in *Alice in Wonderland*."

"Don't forget that Alice fell into a hole. And then there was that bit with the mean Queen of Hearts. You're in for trouble. Don't say I didn't warn you."

Robin could hear her sister roll over, fluff her pillow and smack it twice, then settle down with a satisfied sigh. Sweet dreams, thought Robin, and thanks for the nightmare I'll probably have tonight. Closing her eyes, she tried to dissolve the image of Ms. Beetroot, the mean Queen of Hearts, ordering, "Off with their heads!"

Chapter Seven

While Ms. Beetroot read aloud to the class, Robin cautiously tore a page from her homework notebook. At the top she printed, IDEAS FOR MS. BEETROOT'S PRESENT. She listed three that she had thought of: a plant, a book, pretty soap. Then, she wrote, WHAT DO YOU THINK?

"Sssst," she hissed across the aisle at Barbara. As Ms. Beetroot turned a page, Robin tossed the folded paper. It bounced on the edge of Barbara's desk and slid to the floor beside

Michael. He quickly leaned over, picked up the paper and looked at the note.

Still, Ms. Beetroot continued to read.

Robin glared at Michael to make him give the note back. He smirked, scribbled something on the page, then carelessly tossed it toward Barbara.

That's when Ms. Beetroot looked up from the novel. She looked at Barbara, held her breath, pointed toward the door and waited. Barbara rose slowly from her desk.

"No!" said Robin suddenly. "It wasn't her. It was me. I . . . " But what could she say? The note lying there on Barbara's desk held the secret of Friday's unbirthday party.

"Whad is id Robid?" growled Ms. Beetroot. "I hab bery liddle patiendce for this dodsense."

"It was my paper, not Barbara's."

"Brig id here."

Robin's heart raced! Her mind scrambled through a minefield of possibilities. Suddenly, she knew what she had to do. In an instant, she grabbed the paper from Barbara's desk and without any hesitation crammed it whole into her mouth and began to chew.

"Robid!" shouted Ms. Beetroot. "Whad in the world – ?"

Everyone in the class gasped in shock. Barbara was frozen where she stood beside the classroom door, her mouth gaped open like a patient in a dentist's chair.

"Mm morry, Ms. Meemroom," mumbled Robin, chewing on the forbidden note and quickly making her way out of the classroom to sit on the red bench where she would await whatever punishment Ms. Beetroot planned. It didn't matter. The unbirthday party was saved!

Chapter Eight

As soon as Robin was in the hall, she removed the soggy paper from her mouth and threw it into the garbage can. She sat on the red bench, her heart still racing. Any moment now, her teacher would storm out of the classroom, thundering words at her and glaring lightning.

But something else happened. Mrs. Williams and her class of twenty-eight grade twos came out of their room in single file, on their way to the gymnasium.

"Go along, grade two. I'll be right behind you." Mrs. Williams sat down on the red bench beside Robin. "You don't need to tell me," she said. "This has something to do with the unbirthday party, doesn't it."

"Yes," said Robin, hanging her head and hoping Mrs. Williams wouldn't ask what had happened.

Ms. Beetroot stepped sternly into the hall. "Whad do you hab do say bor yourself, young lady?" She clutched a ball of tissue tightly in the palm of her hand.

Mrs. Williams tried to come to Robin's rescue. Just the smallest hint of a smile was tickling the corners of her mouth. "I'm sure there is a reasonable explanation. After all, Robin has been a very good student all her years here at Ernest Lee. Please do not be too harsh, Ms. Beetroot." Then, she hurried away in the direction of the gymnasium.

Robin did not look up. She waited for punishment to rain down on her.

"You will call your barends at ndoond. You will exblaind this whole badder. Thend we'll bake plands for an endire week of dedentions all dnoondhour. Beanwhile, you cad sid on this red bendch and be silend."

In the deserted hallway, Robin's mind filled with fear and doubt. This was going to mean trouble, big trouble – Queen of Hearts trouble. Make friends with Ms. Beetroot? Impossible! Crazy!

Chapter Nine

An hour later, Robin and Ms. Beetroot were in the principal's office, dialing the number to Robin's home. Even though she had thought and thought, sitting there on that red bench, she came up with nothing to avoid ruining the unbirthday plans.

After three rings, the answering machine clicked on and Robin heard her *own* voice on the tape saying, "You have reached the residence of . . . " Suddenly she had an idea. It was risky, but it just might work.

Pasting an I'm-sorry look on her face, Robin began to speak into the phone. "Mom? It's me. Robin. I got into some trouble and I'm supposed to tell you what I did. Ms. Beetroot is here if you want to talk to her . . . No? Okay, then, I'll explain. Well, I was writing a get-well card for Ms. Beetroot . . . Yeah, she has a real bad cold. So I was getting people to sign it and then Michael threw it at Barbara and she was going to be in trouble so I said it was mine and then I ate it because I didn't want Ms. Beetroot to see it before we all signed it."

Robin saw the look on Ms. Beetroot's face melt from thunder to wonder. The plan was working.

"I know it was wrong, Mom, but we all felt bad when Ms. Beetroot had to miss school, so ... Okay, I will . . . Okay, thanks Mom. Are you sure you don't need to speak to Ms. Beetroot?... Okay, then. Bye."

"Why Robid! I . . . I'b . . ." Ms. Beetroot held a tissue to her red nose, blew gently, and sniffed.

"I'm sorry I ruined the surprise," said Robin. "And I'm sorry I ate the get-well card like that. I know I shouldn't have tried to get people to sign it while you were reading to us. We just thought it would make you feel better."

"Oh dear," said Ms. Beetroot. She drew a fresh tissue from the pocket of her cardigan sweater, touched the corners of her eyes, and smiled a small, very small, smile.

Robin smiled back.

Chapter Ten

On Thursday night, Robin and her grandfather rummaged in the cupboards for flour, sugar, baking powder, cocoa, vanilla, and salt. They rooted in the fridge for eggs, butter, and milk. The mixing bowl, a measuring cup, the wooden spoon, and a baking pan were sitting in a line on the counter.

"Used to make big cakes like this on *The Lady Drake* goin' from Halifax to Barbados," said her grandfather, sifting the flour in a dusty cloud into the largest bowl. "Cooked for eighteen men on that boat and never heard a complaint. Not once. Now, you mix that cocoa up with that sugar and half that butter. Real smooth, now."

They worked and worked, filling the kitchen with warm chocolate smells. When the unbirthday cake was cooled and iced, Robin arranged tiny jellybeans to spell SURPRISE MS. BEETROOT on the top.

Carefully, Robin carried the cake and the present to the bus stop on Friday morning. Carefully, she hid behind Michael and snuck the cake and the present into Mrs. Williams' classroom where they would be safe until the surprise party that afternoon.

Ever since Wednesday and the "phone call," Ms. Beetroot was not quite the same. All her rules were still posted on the door, on the blackboard and beside the pencil sharpener, but they didn't seem to glare down with the same threat as before. During reading, if there was a funny part in the novel, Ms. Beetroot almost laughed. In arithmetic class, when Michael explained the game the substitute teacher had invented, she let him show her how to play.

Even though everyone had to be quiet, the game was still fun.

Soon it was two o'clock and time for the party plans to be put into action.

Mrs. Williams appeared at the door and tapped lightly. "I'm sorry to disturb your lesson, Ms. Beetroot, but you are wanted on the telephone. I'm told it is not an emergency. But if you'd like to take the call, I could look in on your class occasionally."

Robin covered her mouth and grinned.

As soon as Ms. Beetroot was out of sight, everyone rushed into action. Streamers were taped in loops to the blackboard and to Ms. Beetroot's desk. Katie's poster, painted in large balloon shapes with glittery letters, seemed to shout SURPRISE! Cookies, sandwiches, and fudge were spread out on the art table, with the unbirthday cake in the center. Barbara stirred the lemonade and poured it into plastic cups.

Finally the unbirthday present was placed grandly on Ms. Beetroot's desk. The box was very small and a bright red bow covered the top entirely.

"Shhhhh. She's coming," Robin warned.

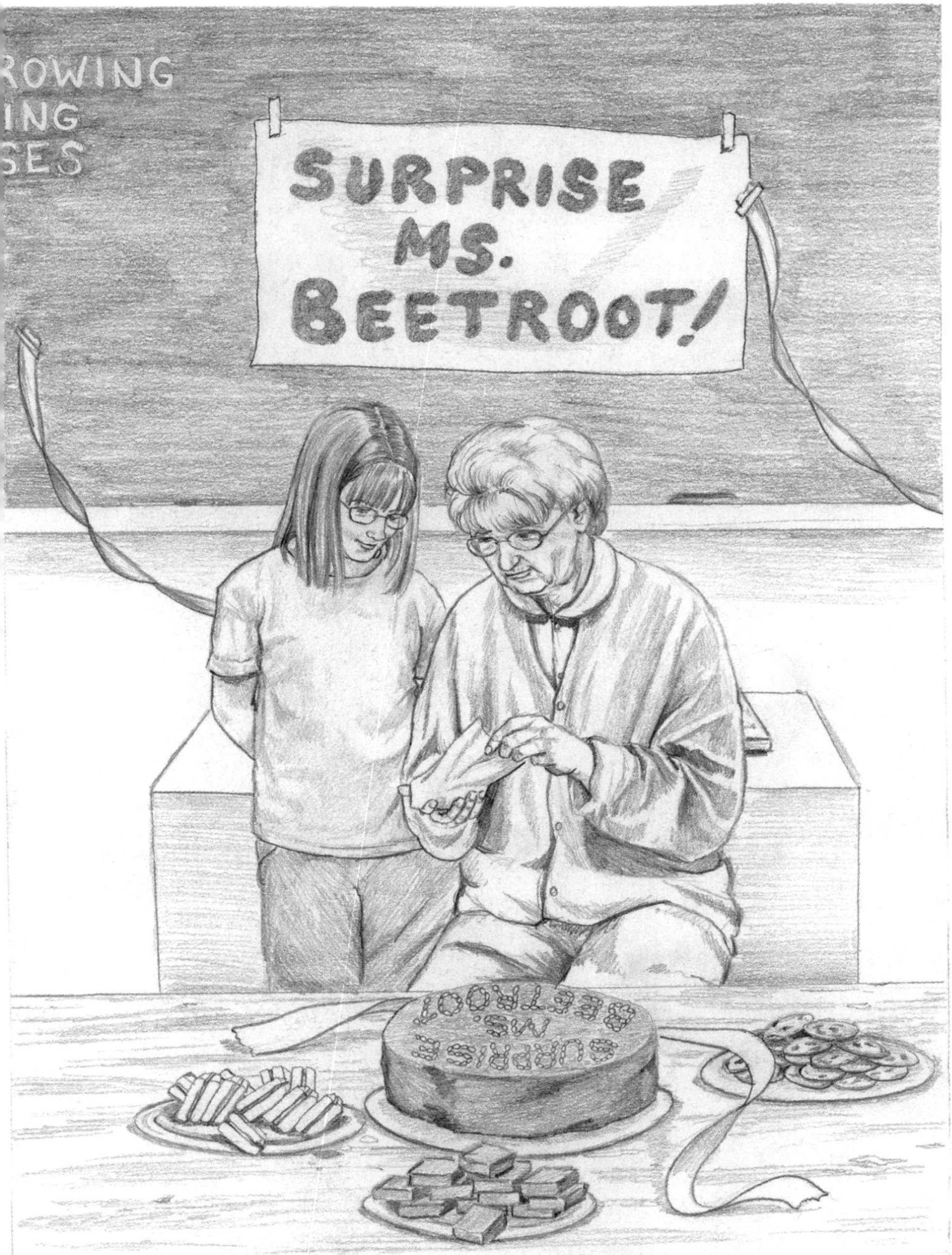
SURPRISE
MS.
BEETROOT!

Everyone waited.

When the doorknob turned and their teacher stepped inside, all the grade fours leapt up and hollered, "Surprise! Happy unbirthday!"

Ms. Beetroot was stunned. Banners? A banquet? Bouncing students? It was almost too much to comprehend.

Robin took Ms. Beetroot's hand and led her to the very small gift that lay waiting to be opened. Everyone gathered closely around.

First the bow was removed and admired. Then, gently, Ms. Beetroot shook the tiny box and listened for any sounds. There were none. The tape was lifted carefully from the red and yellow wrapping paper. The lid was removed from the very small box. She looked inside. "Oh, dear," she said softly. A small smile pulled at the corners of her mouth.

There lay a silver brooch in the shape of an apple. On it was inscribed: *Ms. B from your grade fours.*

"Oh dear," she said again, fastening the brooch to her cardigan sweater.

Suddenly a musical tap-tappity-tap sounded on the classroom door. There stood Mr. Cunningham.

Covering his nose was a bright red rubber ball and disguising his bald head was a tangled purple wig. On his feet were oversized boots with flapping green toes.

"Mrs. Williams has invited me to your unbirthday party to entertain you with my magic. Let the show begin!" he shouted, pulling a long silky scarf out of his sleeve and letting it flutter lightly across his arm. From beneath the scarf, he took one orange, one apple, and one pear.

All the grade fours squealed in delight, clapping and cheering. Ms. Beetroot touched her finger tips against her lips and said, "Oh, dear. Oh, dear," until her smile widened into a broad grin.

Robin sipped lemonade and devoured some delicious chocolate cake as she watched Mr. Cunningham's amazing tricks. Their ordinary classroom wasn't ordinary anymore. It was magic! And Robin knew it had all started with her impossible, crazy idea.

At the end of the day, Mr. Cunningham and Ms. Beetroot stood on the steps smiling and waving goodbye. Robin turned back for one last wave as the yellow bus rumbled out of the schoolyard. To her surprise, she saw Ms. Beetroot tossing the apple and then the orange and then the pear up into the air. Mr. Cunningham reached to rescue them before they crashed to the ground. Ms. Beetroot was beginning to try the juggling act again just as the bus rounded the corner and the school disappeared from sight.

"Ms. Beetroot, a juggler? That's crazy! Impossible!" said Robin to herself. Then she grinned, settled back in her seat, and whistled happily.